W9-BXX-694

First published in the United States, Great Britain, Australia, and New Zealand
in 1994 by North-South Books, an imprint of Nord-Süd Verlag.

Copyright © 1993 by Michael Neugebauer Verlag AG
First published in Switzerland under the title Ich wünscht' ich wär . . . ein Mäuschen.
by Michael Neugebauer Verlag AG, Gossau Zurich.

All rights reserved. No part of this book may be reproduced or utilized in any form
or by any means, electronic or mechanical, including photocopying,
recording, or any information storage and retrieval system,
without permission in writing from the publisher.

Distributed in the United States by North-South Books, Inc., New York.

Library of Congress Cataloging-in-Publication Data is available
A CIP catalogue record for this book is available from The British Library
ISBN 1-55858-344-0 (trade edition)   10 9 8 7 6 5 4 3 2 1
ISBN 1-55858-345-9 (library edition)   10 9 8 7 6 5 4 3 2 1

Printed in Belgium

A Michael Neugebauer Book

NORTH-SOUTH BOOKS / NEW YORK / LONDON

I Wish I Were...
a Mouse

By Eve Tharlet

Haven't you done this yet?

Aren't you finished with that?

Arthur,
put away that lollipop!
Have you picked up your toys?

Have you made your bed?

Don't bite your fingernails!

Don't sit there staring at the television!

If I were a mouse,
everything would be different!

Whoopee!

I would find a nice cake...

and nibble away.

I'd live with my toys
and do nothing but play.

I'd never need to make my bed,

'Cause I'd sleep in a cozy slipper instead.

I'd bite all my nails off just for fun,

And never be scolded by anyone.

I'd plop myself down
right in front of the screen,
And watch for ten hours—
or maybe fifteen!

Yes, Arthur,
but if you were a little mouse,
don't you think you might be
a tiny bit scared...

of the CAT?

Hmmm...

Now, you silly goose,
it's not so bad to be
a little boy after all, is it?

So come along, Arthur.

Let's go and put your toys away.